TWO GENTLEMEN
AND A LADY

Two Gentlemen and a Lady

by

Alexander Woollcott

illustrations by Edwina

Short Story Index Reprint Series

BOOKS FOR LIBRARIES PRESS

FREEPORT, NEW YORK

First Published 1928

Reprinted 1970

INTERNATIONAL STANDARD BOOK NUMBER:

0-8369-3714-7

LIBRARY OF CONGRESS CATALOG CARD NUMBER:

79-134984

PRINTED IN THE UNITED STATES OF AMERICA

To Neysa Moran McMein,
who was a warm personal
friend of most of the
characters in this book,
it is hereby dedicated by

The Author

CONTENTS

THE PASSING OF NICHOLAS

THE PASSING
OF NICHOLAS

Pleasant Lanes, Long Island
November twelfth

Y DEAR ARTHUR:

It will doubtless surprise you to receive a letter from me and indeed I suspect that when our generation passes on and its *Lives and Letters* begin to elbow Stevenson's on the shelf, it will be learned with a publisher's dismay that nowadays brothers communicate with each other only by wire. Of course I used to get news of mine from Mother, but I think it was one of the puzzling shadows on her declining years that she had to serve thus as a clearing house of information for her far flung family. Somehow she felt it was her fault that her three sons were not living together somewhere in inextricable fraternity.

I do hear from Laurence occasionally when something comes up about my investments—either of them. And then, as executor, he writes me annually, as he doubtless does you, inclosing a check which Madame dips into her home-made vocabulary to describe as "a mere pitifance." Laurence's almost surly notes, with their T. R. B./L. K. and their gratuitous "Dictated but not read," always discomfit me.

Not that your own communications, though less formal, are any chummier. By exact count there have been two in the last three years. Of course personally I didn't at all mind the levity of your telegram at the time of our marriage, though it did ruffle Madame a bit, for she seems to resent far more than I do any reference to me as a member of the Only Their Second Husbands Club. When she thinks about it at all, she really sets an immoderately large store by my little doctorate and my lectureship at Columbia. She was so entranced with all my scholastic trappings at Commencement that I suspect she thought I had been produced by Mr. Belasco. Her delight over the floridity of my academic hoods was tinged only by a visible regret that I had never gone in for science and so could not aspire to that hood which makes the chemistry men so closely resemble Chinese sunsets.

But I was a little abashed when I ventured to send you some stray opera seats and asked if you could use them and you replied "Yes—and others. A. K." This seemed so terse and dismissive that I gave up. But now, preposterous as it may seem, I want something of you. I want a dog.

Not just any dog. I suppose I could buy *any* dog myself, though I wouldn't know exactly how to go about it. I have considered the matter at some length from the other side of one of those windows which display the most amusing but the most baffling mass of turbulent puppies. I wonder vaguely how any one can

say of such and such misshapen lump that it will eventually turn into a mastiff or a French poodle. So, suppressing a strong impulse to buy the whole windowful and watch developments, I turn away empty-leashed.

What I want is a fine blooded animal, not necessarily full-grown but possibly able already to help about the premises and certainly already defined in character and general outline. I want a dog that will like me and hate strangers and serve as a watchdog. These suburbs seem like swarming anthills compared with the lonely old place where you and I were brought up, but, after all, our house is pretty much out of earshot and when I'm off lecturing fatuously at the other end of the country and Madame is resting here between tours, I should like to be able to think that she has a staunch and terrifying protector of some sort.

Besides, it would be pleasant to have at least one animal in this place that I could respect amid all the monstrous collection Madame has gradually acquired. . . . I will say that none of them represents her deliberate choice in domestic companions. She hasn't wantonly gone out into the fields and caught them; she has merely caught them the way people catch colds. So when I decided to present her with a dog for her birthday, I made up my mind he should be expertly chosen. That explains this letter to you. You were the first person I thought of.

I'm not sure why I feel so convinced that the choice of a Government bond should be left to Laurence but the choice of a dog to you. The deference may derive from some school-yard memory. Or perhaps it's merely because you live at an athletic club which I dimly picture as a group of horsey bachelors sitting around in thick-soled shoes and talking about the races at Louisville. Anyway, I leave it all to you for I am entirely vague about the various breeds. Only I beg you to be expeditious for I want him installed in full charge of the estate in time to welcome Madame when she returns from her tour. That will be in three weeks' time. She has been having a tremendous success, as you may have read in the papers.

Your affectionate brother

DAVID KENDERDINE

Pleasant Lanes,
Long Island,
November sixteenth

My Dear Arthur:

An Airedale sounds fine. I haven't the faintest notion what one might be like and I didn't know it was possible to pay $500 for a dog—that is, not for one you didn't mean to exhibit at Madison Square Garden but just wanted for use around the place like a gardener. However, I'm quite willing and am inclosing a check for the amount. If I were Laurence, I would write "1 incl." down in the corner, though what good it would do, I'm sure I don't know.

I shan't show your letter to Madame when she comes home. Of course, every one calls her that, not merely the servants and the stage-hands. I'm afraid she wouldn't be at all amused at your little shaft shot in her direction. I do admit she is just the kind who would start a *ménage* and end with a menagerie. But what you don't realize is that she has splendor, which is far rarer and far more delightful than common sense. What you don't understand is that for me, just living with her is a continuously exciting adventure. You've had adventures all your life and so, when you marry, it will be to some one placid and tranquil. I've had nothing but tranquillity since the day I was born and now I shall have excitement as long as I live. Here I was this afternoon, scheduled for some work among my books on mediaeval poisons, but all I could do was just sit and conjure up the vision of her return, her radiant return, with her arms full of

flowers and handbags and her heavy-laden maid struggling after and that absurd How Cum yip-yipping in her wake.

How Cum is part of her menagerie. It IS a menagerie. There is just this one dog—Madame swears he's a dog—who usually goes with her on her travels and is fed, I should imagine, from her make-up box. He is, I am told, a Pekingese. He was finally named How Cum after a strong minority report submitted by me in favor of his being called Ah Gwan. As far as I can see, How Cum simply does not cerebrate at all, though there is just the trace of malicious, sagacious premeditation in the way he invariably flings himself roguishly on my croquet ball and pushes it out of position. I hadn't meant to mention that I have taken up croquet—but there, the damage is done and anyway, there's no reason why, at your age, you should give up a lifelong habit of laughing at me.

Every one seems to have these celestial absurdities and what puzzles me is where they come from or rather

where they were when we were young and those ster-
torous pugs were sliding off the laps of all American
aunts. The pugs have vanished and somehow these
Pekingese have come out of space to take their place.
Surely no one would seriously pretend there were two
of them on the Ark. That would, I think, be carrying
a little *too* far the modern tendency to belittle the
past. Perhaps they sneaked out when John Hay ordered the Open Door but I am more inclined to the
theory that they sprang full-grown from the brow of
some Burbank of the kennels. I'm sure How Cum was
made in a retort, by crossing a muff and a chrysan-
themum.

Then there's Gooseberry. Gooseberry is a cat, a prac-
tically perfect Persian; a soft, gray beauty with no
human affections to speak of. He is dignified and full
of years, for Madame got him long before she acquired
me. He is incapable of emotion, or was until How
Cum came, when he developed an unmistakable aver-
sion, a fine disdain which makes quite a bond between

us. I think it is How Cum's hobbledehoy, rattle-pated lack of restraint which offends Gooseberry so deeply. It's just well-bred disapproval that you see expressed in every uprising hair on Gooseberry's body as he looks

down from the piano on the meaningless antics which fill How Cum's empty life. Poor How Cum, he has no memory at all and as Gooseberry has no heart, he comes to grief every day. It is only because he has been away now on tour for several weeks that his usually unguarded nose will have a chance to heal.

Our birds aren't much. There's a cheap little Sixth Avenue canary given to Madame by some admirer. Her name is Toot Sweet. Then there's a hoarse and despondent old parrot with an insulting laugh whom Madame named Mr. Benchley in a moment of pique. We have two very handsome and patrician but unresponsive goldfish named Hamilton and Stuyvesant respectively, for reasons which I suppose must be obvious. Then there's Charley Young.

Charley Young is a cat—a lean, black-and-white desperado from Chinatown. Madame was motoring down there last spring in an effort to show some southern visitors the sights of the city. I suppose it was really her gracious way of being rude to them—the mere assumption that they would enjoy such a tour. The car was worming its way in gingerly fashion through the crowded streets when this gaunt and alarming creature sprang on the running board and stayed there. I started to shoo him off but Madame intervened in real agitation. I gathered that his advent, or perhaps the manner of it, had some superstitious significance to her. The people of the theater are full

of such ancient pangs and panic. At all events, she ceremoniously installed him out here where Gooseberry has ignored him utterly and where Mr. Benchley destroys his afternoon naps by calling him in a voice most seductively like Madame's. I can't say I blame him for going out a good deal.

THE PASSING OF NICHOLAS

Mrs. Lorrequer, our next-door neighbor, insists that Charley Young has ruined her young Tabby, but I have tried to explain to her delicately that long since we had forehandedly taken the conventional steps to render impossible any such social complications.

You can see over what a helpless world your Airedale will be expected to rule. I shall call him Nicholas after President Butler, who has a somewhat similar position at Columbia.

Your affectionate brother
DAVID KENDERDINE

Pleasant Lanes,
Long Island,
November twenty-seventh

MY DEAR ARTHUR:

This is just a line of thanks to let you know that Nicholas has arrived, that he is superb and that we are already great friends. He came the other morning, escorted on a leash from the kennels by a soiled, aromatic and singularly villainous looking fellow named Doak. Doak assured me that he—Nicholas—had been especially trained as a watchdog. I didn't know dogs *could* matriculate in such a course, but he explained that in all the dogs in Nicholas's class, there had been scientifically and patiently inculcated a distrust of tramps and a fine impulse to fly at the throats of all suspicious-looking characters.

It seems that for an astonishingly small considera-

THE PASSING OF NICHOLAS

tion there are men who consent to don the conventional tatters and allow the kennel people to sic these novices on them—a hazardous calling, I should think. I shall tell Professor Sumpter to include it in his lecture on dangerous trades. I found it difficult to believe, however, that any dog which had grown as attached as Nicholas obviously was to such a fellow as Doak could ever thereafter feel the slightest tinge of distrust of any one in human form.

But I was quite wrong. Nicholas has a vociferous objection to all intruders and becomes excited at the mere thought that a casual passerby may decide after all to come in and see us. He chased the butcher's boy down the drive and half way up the block and we shall have to keep him chained a good deal of the time. I half suspect that his hostility is bogus, that if any stranger would just stand and speak affably to him, Nicholas would stop his rumpus and be demonstratively affectionate on the spot. But as no one has yet thought to try this, I cannot be sure.

Until I can get a decent kennel built for him, he is sleeping indoors and each morning he comes to my room to wake me up. He has the most engaging custom of bringing me a matutinal offering of some sort, anything he can grab up and bear in triumph to my bedside, the while his short tail waves in a gallant

though hopeless attempt to resemble the tossing plume of Navarre. This morning he brought me a dead mouse. It had been Charley Young's trophy, Cook told me later, but evidently Nicholas thought I should have it. He smuggled it into my bed, but his intentions were generous.

Dogs are fine, large-hearted creatures anyway. Nicholas's spirit, for instance, is far finer and, in the best sense, more human than Mrs. Lorrequer's. Yesterday, I rocked abstractedly on his foot. It must have hurt like the very devil yet he not only didn't show resentment, as you would have done, but fairly flung himself on me in his eagerness to show that he quite understood how it had happened. There was I, feeling sorry for him and he feeling sorry for me and it was all very fraternal and pleasant. That time when, with equal innocence, I emptied a pail of water out of my window and you chanced to be sauntering underneath, your reaction, as I now bitterly recall it, was totally dissimilar to Nicholas's splendid understanding.

I regret to have to inform you that Mrs. Lorrequer was quite right about Charley Young. Of the five kittens born to Mrs. Lorrequer's Lucile, four look so exactly like the old rounder I find under my patronage, that my denial faltered on my lips when first I saw them. This was when they were plumped down, mother and all, on my verandah by the Lorrequer chauffeur,

who also delivered an oral message to the effect that she was sure they would fit very nicely into our establishment. I had the pleasure of seeing Nicholas chase the fellow home. I wish he could have had a chance at Mrs. Lorrequer.

I called her up but she did not permit me to pursue the conversation to a satisfactory conclusion. I tried a weak jest about an unexpected triumph of love over science but she only snorted. I then ventured to explain that there had probably been some carelessness or misunderstanding at the veterinary's and as she seemed to unbend a little, I offered handsomely to have Charley Young make an honest cat of Lucile. At that point, she hung up.

I had a great deal of work to do to-day, but none of it is done, for I have spent the whole afternoon trying to think up appropriate names for the progeny of Charley Young. At present, I have decided to call them Brigham, Roland, Clara Kimball, Rida Johnson and Only-the-good-die Young. I am now considering a new name for Lucile. It will be confusing to call her Mrs. Charley Young and besides it would be against Madame's principles in such matters.

Madame will reach home next week. Of course I have said nothing about Nicholas in my letters to her which is probably why I have had to let off steam about him in this unwonted garrulity towards you. However, you won't be bothered by many more letters from me, for Madame is coming home. You would laugh if you knew how that prospect excites

Your affectionate brother

DAVID KENDERDINE

Pleasant Lanes, Long Island
December second

MY DEAR ARTHUR:

This is just to let you know that your Airedale has been a disaster, that he and I and, probably, you are in disgrace and that one of us, at least, is in danger of banishment. The little gift you so kindly helped me prepare for Madame as a surprise on her return has been all of that.

43

TWO GENTLEMEN AND A LADY

It happened, unfortunately, in my absence. I had gone into New York bright and early to meet her, misunderstood her train time, waited forlornly around the Pennsylvania station for an hour, learned my mistake, realized that she must be already here and hurried back home only to find the place in an uproar. The doctor's car was just whirling out of the drive as I reached the corner. Charley Young was perched immovable in the highest tree, where, apparently, he intends to spend his old age. Mr. Benchley, minus several of the feathers he had most highly prized, was swearing with a flavor and fecundity he must have learned at sea. And Gooseberry, who was responsible for Mr. Benchley's depression, had retired to the mantelpiece in mingled wrath and satisfaction. Madame, with How Cum clutched to her bosom, was upstairs recovering from recurrent hysterics.

After a while, from the agitated tales told by her maid and Cook, I reconstructed what had happened. She had arrived, bag and baggage, a little before noon,

and swept up the path, a vision to behold with all the flowers and impedimenta and camp-followers that are part of her progress through the world. Of course she called to me, being sure I must be desperately ill not to have met her at the station. But it was not I who responded. It was Nicholas. He hurried conscientiously out, took one look, and bit her.

I shouldn't have tried to explain—or, at least, not right away. Making a hesitant approach to her room, I mistakenly urged her to be reasonable. I pointed out that the poor fellow had only done what he was laboriously and expensively trained to do. "I thought as much," she said, very tartly. "It was an exquisite jest." And relapsed in a manner so alarming that I was obliged to tiptoe from the room.

I am afraid now that she will insist upon my giving him away, which, I don't mind telling you, would desolate me beyond expression. To be sure, she has not suggested this. That is partly because her door has been locked for four hours and partly, I am afraid, because she has not yet progressed beyond her first idea of having him shot at sunrise.

My great hope is that before any such Tudor edict can be carried out, I will have been able to untrain him—or is the word detrain?—from his habit of flying at strangers. I think the idea is really foreign to his nature and that it would not be difficult to dislodge it. Indeed, he was already quite discouraged about his career when I went out to the garage to talk it all over with him. He almost uprooted his ring from the concrete at the mere sight of a friendly face and it was perfectly apparent to a dispassionate observer that he was fully aware of something having gone wrong. He knew he hadn't been a success. Late this afternoon, when Mrs. Lorrequer went snippily by, and his instinct bade him at least go forth and roar at her through the palings, a single fierce word from me kept him quivering and abashed at my side. This could not have happened yesterday.

Now I am wondering if I could not teach him a few

tricks that would disarm the opposition. To this end I have been laboring faithfully all afternoon and I even went so far as to cut my lecture at Columbia, partly because I wanted to concentrate on this new scheme and partly for fear some word of all this unpleasantness might have drifted as far as the Faculty Club. At all events, I spent most of the afternoon trying to teach him to bring in the evening paper. I may say I think I *have* taught him. At five every afternoon a small boy tucks *The Evening Post* or whatever it is into every gate in our street and I think it would be pleasant if it were an established part of Nicholas's duties to bring ours to my desk.

I suppose Mr. Doak would have known just how to suggest this to him, but I didn't. I finally hit upon the scheme of inserting the folded paper between his jaws, clamping them together and dragging him to the library. This did not work so very well at first, but this was because Nicholas, while quite pathetically eager to enter into the spirit of any project of mine, misun-

derstood the present purpose. He thought the game was a tug-of-war and into the spirit of that he entered with gusto. He would sit down emphatically, rather in the manner of a dirt cart being dumped, and would be humorously dogged, which, come to think of it, must be the source of the word, though it had never occurred to me before. However, I'm stronger than Nicholas, so he would always end up, together with a good deal of gravel, in the library, where I would reward him with some meat. We repeated this maneuver eight or nine times and now I think he understands. At least I saw him a moment ago out sniffing the garden gate as if hoping for another bit of newsprint with which to redeem himself.

I have telephoned the doctor, partly to urge him to say nothing about this misadventure of Madame's, which might sound funny if unsympathetically recounted and partly to learn how seriously she had been hurt. Not seriously, at all, it seems, except from shock. The gardener says the path will have to be relaid and indeed, there is quite a trench worn by Nicholas's lessons. Cook says I shall get only an omelette for dinner because of my having given every scrap of meat in the larder to Nicholas in the course of his instruction. However, things do look brighter. We must hope for the best—he and I.

Your affectionate brother
DAVID KENDERDINE

Pleasant Lanes, Long Island
December third

MY DEAR ARTHUR:

Well, the skies have cleared and Nicholas has been accepted. He entertained Madame so much to-day that I don't at all mind its having been at my expense. It seems that all yesterday afternoon she had been watching from her window our struggles over the evening paper, and I gather that, from that elevation, these were rather amusing. I found that out this afternoon when she asked me with withering skepticism whether I thought my little plan had finally been adopted by Nicholas. Nervously, I decided to put him to the test.

"Nicholas Murray," I said sternly, "go get me *The Evening Post*." He raced out and returned in two minutes with the paper between his teeth and his pleased

head tossing like a poplar in a storm. Of course I accepted it casually, slipped him a cookie and tried not to gloat too openly over Madame's discomfiture. Then

THE PASSING OF NICHOLAS

Nicholas looked at me roguishly, dashed out of the house and returned shortly with another copy—one marked Lorrequer. That was the cue for Madame's first public smile since her return. By five o'clock, she was in immense good humor. All told, Nicholas brought in three *Posts*, four *Suns* and two *Brooklyn Eagles*.

Of course, the neighbors soon had us on the telephone and I understand that the Pleasant Lanes operator became extremely sarcastic over the simultaneous effort of every house in our street to call us. It took me some time to get all the papers restored and all the neighbors soothed and I had to cut my seminar at the university but it was all worth it. Nicholas was

being restored at the same time. Madame said he was "priceless," which word was the only treasure she succeeded in sneaking past the customs men on her return from England last summer.

Charley Young came down from the tree this morning. He looks greatly aged. I imagine that you won't be hearing again from me for some time.

Your affectionate brother
DAVID KENDERDINE

Pleasant Lanes, Long Island
April third

My Dear Arthur:

I am writing you after a long silence to see if you have the time and the inclination to select and send me another dog. I am not particular as to the breed and training, for I have become convinced that somehow I am able to mold a dog's character and tendencies into any form I think best. Of course I need not stipulate that nothing of the Pekingese variety would be acceptable. A decently sizable dog is my preference. One of the most endearing things about Nicholas the Absurd was his perverse habit of trying to take forty winks in a small rocker drawn to the scale of How Cum. His ever expanding bulk would protrude from, and overflow, the chair in all directions, his tail and his forelegs and even his troglodyte head drooping from it like a weeping willow tree out of drawing.

I am afraid I have already let slip the fact that Nicholas is no longer with us. I did give some thought to the possibilities of an evasion on this point but it did not seem feasible. I admit feeling hesitant to tell the story because it does seem, however unjustly, to reflect on me. And it is quite true that the manner of his going can be traced directly to my earnest and, as the event proved, spectacularly successful effort to

break him of his watchdog proclivities. Indeed, it took very little ingenuity and no great amount of time to destroy utterly all the snobbish provincialism of his notions about the distinctions to be drawn between the Kenderdines and the rest of society.

All went well until we closed the place for the winter or rather set it ajar while we came into town for the coldest weeks. A budding romance between Cook and the gardener, having resulted in marriage, provided us providentially with caretakers and thus the greater part of the menagerie was left to enjoy the winter sports in Pleasant Lanes. The idea of confining Nicholas to our tiny hotel suite in New York was never seriously entertained, though I knew he would grieve for us and I used occasionally to pretend I had left some rare book out here at the house just for an excuse to drive out and hear the wild music of his greeting. At the end of these brief visits, however, the separation was doubly painful and all the way back to town I would be haunted by the expression on Nicholas's face as it was visible to the last, glued to the window-pane and incredulous at the baseness of such desertion.

Well, one afternoon last week just before we were scheduled for the spring migration to the country, some muscular strangers drove up to Pleasant Lanes with a truck of honest and convincing appearance and, at their leisure, removed all the best things in our house. To be precise, they carried off a Sixteenth Century Rhineland wedding chest filled with linen, six bottles of red Chateauneuf-du-Pape, one considerable painting, a few good etchings and a grand piano.

The details of this robbery were first imparted to me over the telephone by Mrs. Lorrequer, who fairly glowed with inner satisfaction at being the bearer of such tidings. The rapine of my house had taken place during the afternoon at an hour, when, in defiance of the most solemn injunctions on the subject, Cook and her still devoted husband repaired jointly to the Pleasant Lanes Picture Palace, leaving the premises under the protection of the indignant Nicholas.

From the window of her own library Mrs. Lorrequer had noted the arrival of the van and, at the sight of chattels leaving, instead of coming to the house, she had been mildly surprised, in so far—she conveyed by her voice—as she could any longer be surprised by anything which might happen in so bizarre a household. At that point I ventured to express the opinion that even so primitive a community sense as seems to animate Pleasant Lanes might have prompted her to investigate. A spoon or two might be smuggled out of my house without arousing her slumbering neighborliness. But a grand piano! Really, Mrs. Lorrequer!

Well, as she thought back on her inaction, it seemed probable that all her suspicions were allayed by the part that Nicholas had played. Nicholas, it seems, had been so frankly delighted by the advent of the robbers that Mrs. Lorrequer had thought of them

vaguely as relations or at least old chums of Madame's. Why, Nicholas had bustled in and out of the house, himself anxiously attending each stolen article on its way to the van and then hurrying back as if to superintend the selection of just the right things to take along on what he evidently regarded as a really splendid picnic.

The last she saw of Nicholas was as the truck was vanishing around the corner of the street on its way to the Merrick Road.

He was sitting on the piano.

Your affectionate brother
DAVID KENDERDINE

THE STORY
OF VERDUN BELLE

THE STORY OF VERDUN BELLE

I FIRST heard the tale of Verdun Belle's adventures as it was being told one June afternoon under a drowsy apple tree in the troubled valley of the Marne.

The story began in a chill, grimy Lorraine village, where, in hovels and haymows, a disconsolate detachment of United States Marines lay waiting the order to go up into that maze of trenches of which the crumbling traces still weave a haunted web around the citadel called Verdun.

TWO GENTLEMEN AND A LADY

Into this village at dusk one day in the early spring of 1918, there came out of space a shabby, lonesome dog—a squat setter bitch of indiscreet, complex and unguessable ancestry. One watching her as she trotted intently along the smelly village street would have sworn that she had an important engagement with the Mayor and was, regretfully, a little late.

At the end of the street she came to where a young buck private lounged glumly on a doorstep. Halting in her tracks, she sat down to contemplate him. Then, satisfied seemingly by what she sensed and saw, she came over and flopped down beside him in a most companionable manner, settling herself comfortably as if she had come at last to her long journey's end. His pleased hand reached over and played with one silken chocolate-colored ear. Somehow that gesture sealed a compact between those two. There was thereafter no doubt in either's mind that they belonged to each other for better or for worse, in sickness and in health, through weal and woe, world without end.

She ate when and what he ate. She slept beside him in the haymow, her muzzle resting on his leg so that he might not get up in the night and go forgetfully back to America without her noticing it. To the uninitiated onlookers her enthusiasm may not have been immediately explicable. In the eyes of his top sergeant and his company clerk he may well have seemed an undistinguished warrior, freckle-faced and immensely indifferent to the business of making the world safe for democracy. But Verdun Belle thought him the most charming person in all the world. There was a loose popular notion that she had joined up with the company as mascot and belonged to them all. She affably let them think so, but she had her own ideas on the subject.

When they moved up into the line she went along and was so obviously trench-broken that they guessed she had already served a hitch with some French regiment in that once desperate region. They even built up the not implausible theory that she had come to them lonely from the grave of some little soldier in faded horizon blue. Certainly she knew trench ways, knew in the narrowest of passages how to keep out from underfoot and was so well aware of the dangers of the parapet that a plate of chicken bones up there would not have interested her. She even knew what

gas was, and after a reminding whiff of it became more than reconciled to the regulation gas mask, which they patiently wrecked for all subsequent human use because an unimaginative War Department had not foreseen the peculiar anatomical specifications of Verdun Belle.

In May, when the outfit was engaged in the exhausting activities which the High Command was pleased to describe as "resting," Belle thought it a convenient time to present an interested but amply forewarned regiment with seven wriggling casuals, some black and white and mottled as a mackerel sky, some splotched with the same brown as her own. These newcomers complicated the domestic economy of the leatherneck's haymow, but they did not become an acute problem until that memorable night late in the month when breathless word bade these troops be up and away.

The Second Division of the A. E. F. was always being thus picked up by the scruff of the neck and flung across France, and it was an inseparable ingredient in their magnificent morale that they always set forth in the touching confidence that they must be on their way to Paris or New York to parade before an enthralled citizenry. This time the enemy had snapped up Soissons and Rheims and were pushing with dreadful ease and speed toward the remembering Marne. Foch was calling upon the Americans to help stem the tide. Ahead of the Marines, as they scrambled across the monotonous plain of the Champagne, there lay amid the ripening wheat fields a mean and hilly patch of timber called Belleau Wood. Verdun Belle went along.

The leatherneck had solved the problem of the puppies by drowning four and placing the other three in a basket he had begged from a village woman. His notion that he could carry the basket would have come as a shock to whatever functionary back in Washington had designed the Marine pack, which, with its neat assortment of food supplies, extra clothing, emergency restoratives and gruesome implements for destruction, was so painstakingly calculated to exhaust the capacity of the human back. But in his need the young Marine somehow contrived to add an item not in the regulations—namely, one basket containing three unweaned and faintly resentful puppies.

By night and by day the troop movement was made, now in little wheezing trains, now in swarming lorries, now afoot. Sometimes Belle's crony rode. Sometimes (under pressure of popular clamor against the

TWO GENTLEMEN AND A LADY

room he was taking up) he would yield up his place
to the basket and jog along with his hand on the tail-
board, while Belle trotted behind him.

All the soldiers in Christendom seemed to be moving across France to some nameless crossroads over

the hill. Obviously this was no mere shift from one quiet sector to another. They were going to war. Every one had assured the stubborn youngster that he would not be able to manage, and now misgivings settled on him like crows.

He guessed that Verdun Belle must be wondering, too. He turned to assure her that everything would be all right. She was not there. Ahead of him, behind him, there was no sign of her. No one within call had seen her quit the line. He kept telling himself she would show up. But the day went and the night came without her.

He jettisoned the basket and pouched the pups in his forest-green shirt in the manner of a motherly kangaroo. In the morning one of the three was dead and the problem of transporting the other two was now tangled by the circumstance that he had to feed them.

An immensely interested old woman in the village where they halted at sunup, vastly amused by this spectacle of a soldier trying to carry two nursing puppies to war, volunteered some milk for the cup of his mess-kit, and with much jeering advice from all sides and by dint of the eye-dropper from his pack, he tried sheepishly to be a mother to the two waifs. The attempt was not shiningly successful.

He itched to pitch them over the fence. But maybe Verdun Belle had not been run over by some thundering camion. If she lived she would find him, and then what would he say when her eyes asked what he had done with the pups? So, as the order was shouted to fall in, he hitched his pack to his back and stuffed his charges back into his shirt. Now, in the morning light, the highway was choked. Down from the lines in agonized, grotesque rout came the stream of French life from the threatened countryside, jumbled fragments of fleeing French regiments inextricably mixed with despairing old folks and little children, dragging or pushing along a goat, perhaps, or a baby-carriage full of dishes or whatever else they had caught up in their flight from the heartsick homes. But America was coming up the road.

It was a week in which the world held its breath. The battle was close at hand now. Field hospitals, jostling in the river of traffic, sought space to pitch their tents. The top sergeant of one such outfit was riding on the driver's seat of an ambulance. Marines in endless number were moving up fast. It was one of these who, in a moment's halt, fell out of line, leaped to the step of the blockaded ambulance, and looked eagerly into the pill-rolling top sergeant's eyes.

"Say, buddy," whispered the youngster, "take care of these for me. I lost their mother in the jam."

The Top found his hands closing on two drowsy pups. He started to hand them back at once but the stranger had stepped down and been swallowed up in the crowd.

All that day the field-hospital personnel was harried by the task of providing nourishment for the two casuals who had been thus unexpectedly attached to them for rations. Once established in a farmhouse (from which they were promptly shelled out), the Top went over the possible provender and found that the pups were not yet equal to a diet of bread, corn sirup and corned willy. A stray cow, loosed from her moorings in the great flight, was browsing tentatively in the next field, and two orderlies who had carelessly reminisced of life on their farms back home were detailed to induce her coöperation. But the bombardment had brought out a certain moody goatishness in this cow, and she would not let them come near her.

THE STORY OF VERDUN BELLE

After a hot and maddening chase that lasted two hours, the two milkmen reported a complete failure to their disgusted chief.

The problem was still unsolved at sundown, and the pups lay faint in their bed of absorbent cotton out in the garden, when, bringing up the rear of a detachment of Marines that straggled past, there trotted a brown-and-white setter.

"It would be swell if she had milk in her," the top sergeant said reflectively, wondering how he could salvage the mascot of an outfit on the march.

But his larcenous thoughts were waste. At the gate she halted dead in her tracks, flung her head high to sniff the air, wheeled sharp to the left and became just a streak of brown and white against the ground. Her sharp, challenging bark was a mess-call, clear and unmistakable. The entire staff came out and formed a jostling circle to watch the family reunion.

After that it was tacitly assumed that these casuals belonged. When the hospital was ordered to shift fur-

ther back beyond reach of the whining shells, Verdun
Belle and the pups were intrusted to an ambulance
driver and went along in style. They all moved—bag,
baggage and livestock—into the deserted little Chateau
of the Guardian Angel, of which the front windows
were curtained against the eyes and dust of the road,
but of which the rear windows looked out across droop-

ing fruit trees upon a sleepy, murmurous, multicolored valley, fair as the Garden of the Lord.

The operating tables, with acetylene torches to light them, were set up in what had been a tool shed. Cots were strewn in the orchard alongside. Thereafter for a month there was never rest in that hospital. The surgeons and orderlies spelled each other at times, snatching morsels of sleep and returning a few hours later to relieve the others. But Verdun Belle took no time off. Between cat naps in the corner, due attentions to her restive brood and an occasional snack for herself, she managed somehow to be on hand for every

ambulance, cursorily examining each casualty as he was lifted to the ground.

Then, in the four o'clock dark of one morning, the orderly bending over a stretcher that had just been rested on the ground was hit by something that half bowled him over. The projectile was Verdun Belle. Every quivering inch of her proclaimed to all concerned that here was a case she was personally in charge of. From nose to tail-tip she was taut with excitement, and a kind of eager whimpering bubbled up out of her as if she ached to sit back on her haunches and roar to the star-spangled sky but was really too busy at the moment to indulge herself in any release so satisfying to her soul. For here was this mess of a leatherneck of hers to be washed up first. So like him to get all dirty the moment her back was turned! The first thing he knew as he came to was the feel of a rough pink tongue cleaning his ears.

I saw them all next day. An ambling passer-by, I came upon two cots shoved together under an apple

tree. Belle and her ravenous pups occupied one of these. On the other the young Marine—a gas case, I think, but maybe his stupor was shell shock and perhaps he had merely had a crack on the head—was deep in a dreamless sleep. Before drifting off he had taken the comforting precaution to reach out one hand and close it tight on a silken ear.

Later that day he told me all about his dog. I doubt if I ever knew his name, but some quirk of memory makes me think his home was in West Philadelphia and that he had joined up with the Marines when he came out of school.

I went my way before dark and never saw them again, nor ever heard tell what became of the boy and his dog. I never knew when, if ever, he was shipped back into the fight, nor where, if ever, those two met again. For a long time it has remained, you see, a story without an end, though there must, I think, be those here and there in this country who had witnessed and could set down for us the chapter that never was written.

I hope there was something prophetic in the closing paragraph of the anonymous account of Verdun Belle which appeared the next week in the A. E. F. newspaper, The Stars and Stripes. That paragraph was a benison which ran in this wise:

"Before long they would have to ship him on to the evacuation hospital, on from there to the base hospital, on and on and on. It was not very clear to any one how another separation could be prevented. It was a perplexing question, but they knew in their hearts they could safely leave the answer to some one else. They could leave it to Verdun Belle."

MY FRIEND EGON

MY FRIEND EGON

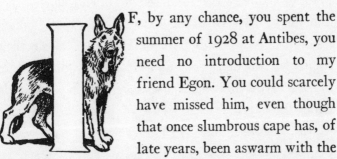F, by any chance, you spent the summer of 1928 at Antibes, you need no introduction to my friend Egon. You could scarcely have missed him, even though that once slumbrous cape has, of late years, been aswarm with the conspicuous. Probably the manager of the Hotel du Cap himself could not tell you why, in obedience to the ever reliable herd instinct of the human species, the drift of the summer tourists turned, a few seasons after

the war, toward his deserted corner of the Riviera. He merely thanks God and rubs his hands.

In the crowd, you must have seen Lloyd Osborne, indistinguishable from a lizard on the sun-baked rocks in front of his terra cotta home. You may have seen Mary Garden or Lily Langtry, perhaps, running over from Monte Carlo to a dinner party at the Cap. You can hardly have escaped the Dwight Deere Wimans (late of Moline, Ill.) and the Archibald MacLeishes and the Charles Bracketts (late of Saratoga), taking up an unconscionable part of the *plage* with their respective young. You doubtless saw Mrs. James Hazen Hyde, bearing up with remarkable fortitude under the continual annoyance of being mistaken for Marie Tempest. And perhaps you even saw Marie Tempest herself. Or Elsie deWolfe (Lady Mendl, to you) throning away in La Garoupe, the largest villa at the Cap. Oh, these, and Montemezzi, perhaps, and Moronzoni, and Walker Ellis of New Orleans, and Benjamin Strong of the Federal Reserve Bank, and

MY FRIEND EGON

(so as to have a little of everything) Dudley Field Malone.

But it is none of these you will remember longest. The unforgettable habitué of Antibes is Egon. He had been wintering and springing in New York, and you might have seen him almost any day that you dropped in at the White Horse Tavern in West 45th Street, where he rather made a point of keeping an eye on the coatroom, being, I think, the only coatroom attendant in town who could dispose of a troublesome customer, or even knock off for the day, merely by executing a neat standing broad jump over the counter. But with the coming of spring to West 45th Street, Egon began to betray a nostalgia for Antibes and made it clear enough that he was obliged to meet a friend over there. Victorio, the coatroom boy at the Algonquin, had left in April for six months of painting in Paris. I shouldn't be at all surprised if Egon got the idea from him.

At that time, Egon still belonged to the younger

generation, having been born as recently as 1921. He is one of the largest and most powerful German police dogs ever bred in the kennels of Berlin. Even when he was very young, he cost as much as a high powered automobile. He was acquired when he was a yearling by Benjamin Ficklin Finney, Jr., sometime student in residence at the University of Virginia and later a Captain in the United States Marines in France where, I need hardly add, he was popularly known as Finney la Guerre.

Benjamin Ficklin Finney, Sr., stays the year round in Sewanee, Tenn., where he is the Regent of the University of the South. Benjamin Ficklin Finney, Jr., having inherited the famous Penelo Plantation at Tarboro, N. C., stays nowhere at all very long and, to put it in a nutshell, does nothing in particular. But, like the House of Lords, he does it very well.

When last heard from in December of 1927, Massa Ben, as the old planter is sometimes called, was on his way into the depths of Indo-China, with a rifle over his shoulder and a commission from the Chicago Field Museum to come out with the pelt of some animal that most stay-at-homes would think of as not really being worth all that trouble. You may possibly have read of Massa Ben in the tabloids, for he has been variously reported, at one time or another, as engaged to most of the celebrated beauties of our time, with the possible exception of Mrs. Leslie Carter. But, for the most part, Finney is as inconspicuous as the husband of some famous star. He is known all over the world merely as that nice-looking young man who owns Egon. Egon, in turn, has an excessively high opinion of the value of his master to society, an opinion tempered, to be sure, by his occasional suspicion that Massa Ben is not quite bright and will probably get drowned in the Mediterranean if Egon is not there to keep an eye on him.

Indeed, Egon's single social gaucherie derives from his arrant assumption that he is the only good swimmer in the world. This made him more than a little

trying when I first met him at Antibes. That was before the days of the great congestion, caused by the comparatively recent notion that all the best people naturally spend the summer in that still somewhat surprised portion of the Riviera. In those days, the silence of the Antibes nights was broken only by the sweet music of the nightingales and the cries of the wounded borne faintly on the wind from the Casino at Juan les Pins. The silence of the mornings was broken only by the sound of Tennessee's own Grace Moore firmly practicing the scales in her pink villa at the Cap.

The honorable Montague Norman, Governor of the Bank of England, would gather his *peignoir* about him, proceed majestically down the leafy footway from the hotel, pause on the rocks for a bit of sun and then cleave the turquoise depths with his venerable person. He might get out quite a distance when Egon would hurry forward, wearing his Drat-the-man-he's-in-again expression. Failing utterly to conceal his deep enjoyment of this further load of responsibility thrown upon him by the incompetence of the human race, he would run out on the springboard, toss up his head in a clamor of scolding and then leap into the sea, heading like a destroyer toward the unsuspecting financier. A little later, a coastful of lazy human molluscs would chuckle at the spectacle of the Honorable Montague Norman being helplessly delivered on shore. I have heard people (in dry-bathing suits) loudly wonder why swimmers thus lent themselves to Egon's palpable exhibitionism. They were foolish, it seems, to let themselves be rescued. I myself used to say the same until the day came when I had grown so dear to him that he just could not bear the thought of my drowning out there in the Mediterranean.

It is quite useless to resist. You know that trick the life guards are taught for use when they must deal with the witless and hampering struggles of a drowning person. The life guard must haul back with his free hand, sock the little struggler on the jaw and

then, undisturbed, tow his unconscious form to shore. It is an old trick along the beaches of the world. Egon learned it early. Of course he does not knock you unconscious. He merely strokes your bare skin with his paws until you shriek with agony, and, in crises, he bites you. You yourself would soon abandon the notion of resistance if you could see this fiend in canine form, only slightly smaller than Man-o'-War, bearing down on you with the resolution of the Twentieth Century Limited and wearing, when you try playfully to evade him, an expression of wordless rage that fairly chills the blood. "Oh, well," you say, "if that's the way you feel about it," and you put a consenting hand on his still angry hackles. At that gesture of surrender, he circles like a wherry and heads for shore, the very throb of his engine suggesting that he could take on a few dozen more fools if need be.

Of course, he himself is no mean swimmer. When urged, he makes a pretty 40 foot dive from the high rocks, first devoting some little time to a preliminary barking, which is part misgivings, part excitement, part sheer showmanship, because it would be so foolish to dive until enough people were looking his way. But in the end he does dive, clean and straight and proud as Lucifer.

And he rides an aquaplane. He cannot mount one unaided, but I have seen Scott Fitzgerald help his floundering efforts to get on. Then Fitzgerald would slip off into the water and Egon would ride alone, balancing expertly and terribly pleased with himself. Indeed, he can circle the bay indefinitely, provided only that Ben Finney is sitting in the motor boat in plain sight. Otherwise, after a minute, you can fairly see Egon's eyes cloud with a worry as to where that fool Finney of his is. Fallen into the water, perhaps, and probably going down for the last time. It is too much. Egon will turn around, scan the sea, lose his balance as a consequence and pitch crestfallen and furious into the water. By the time he comes up for air, the motor boat is half way to Cannes.

MY FRIEND EGON

There was a period when serious thought was given to the notion of starring Egon in the movies in order that, in the course of time, he might succeed the aging Rin Tin Tin as John Barrymore succeeded Forbes-Robertson. Indeed, once when he was spending the winter in Florida a few years ago, he wandered impromptu into a picture that the late Barbara La Marr was making there and came close to running away with her triumph. It was quite evident that (in the pattern of the favorite Hollywood bedtime story) he could easily step from movie extra to star overnight. If nothing came of this project, I suspect it was because the roving Finney would not stay in one country long enough to let Egon have a career.

Probably it is just as well, for Hollywood compels its dog stars to perform only the most routine heroics, and a really interesting scenario—something that Egon could have got his teeth into, as I believe the actors phrase it—would never have been suffered to reach the production stage.

TWO GENTLEMEN AND A LADY

Consider, for instance, the discouragement which was the portion of Herman J. Mankiewicz, an artistically ambitious underling in the Famous Players forces, when he tried to write a character part for Rin Tin Tin. The scenario, which was icily rejected, was called "The Idiot Rin Tin Tin." It was to open on a scene of skurrying clouds and wind-tossed trees and, at last, the gaunt hound himself standing on a rocky crag, his magnificent figure silhouetted against the sunset. Then his great head was to lift inquiringly, apprehensively, as if the wind had borne him the first faint scent of danger. He was to turn swiftly, see a movement in the underbrush and, all of a sudden, descry a rabbit looking at him with alarming severity. A pause, a trembling, a dropping of the tail and the idiot Rin Tin Tin was to run for dear life.

Next, you were to see him with his master, the village drunk, who would kick and abuse him horribly, but whom he seemed to adore all the more on that account. And you would follow the story until, in

TWO GENTLEMEN AND A LADY

Rin Tin Tin's absence, villains were to fall upon his master and lash the fellow to a railroad track in the path of an oncoming express. Then would follow one of those breath-taking races between the forces of good and evil. You were to see the poor wretch writhing in a vain effort to loose his bonds. You were to see the huge train rushing down the valley. Ten miles away—nine miles away—eight miles away. Would help come in time? Would no one intervene to save him? On would come the great Limited—a roar of wheels in the silence, a streak of light in the night.

Then, over in the village, you were to see Rin Tin Tin rise from his nap, shake himself, prick up his ears, wheel suddenly in his tracks and race out into the fields. You were to watch the two converge on the helpless fellow lashed to the ties—the belching train, hurling itself around curves, the racing dog, with lolling tongue and ears straight back, hurrying across the fields. Six miles away——five miles away—four miles away. He might be in time. He must be in time. He

MY FRIEND EGON

would be in time. Just before the train could enter its last stretch, Rin Tin Tin would sweep up to the rail bed, dart straight to the spot where his master lay bound—and, since he never would have a better opportunity, bite him.

That was the Mankiewicz idea, and it was rejected. The depressed scenarist might still be willing to remain identified with an art form so servile to the box-office and the movies may well have been good enough for the unexacting Rin Tin Tin. But I am sure they were no career for Egon.

Nor would the spoken drama—I suppose he would call it the barking stage—beckon to Egon urgently in this generation. Though still in his prime, he shares to the full that pessimism about the theater which usually comes only with the hardening of the arteries. The stage, he feels, is not what it used to be. Time was when a dog with red blood could always get a job chasing Liza across the ice. But they don't produce plays like that any more. When, for a sentimental relic called "Palmy Days," which he produced a few years ago, Arthur Hopkins needed a fine, emotional dog of the old school, he found that the breed had died out or, at least, had become as rare as an actress who could play Camille. Finally, for lack of a plausible bloodhound, Mr. Hopkins gave up the attempt at typecasting and engaged a young mastiff from the provinces. The young mastiff's performance lacked that certain something. He was supposed to be first heard baying in the distance and then come charging on, pushing his way furiously through the crowd and plunging straight at the neck of the villain, as a trout leaps at a fly. The mastiff did the offstage baying part adequately, but he did not plunge on. He strolled on, yawning. Wilton Lackaye—another cutup in the same troupe—named him Atlantic City forthwith, because of his bored walk. Egon would have done better than this, but the stage, I think, is not for him.

As the spring of 1928 began to wane, it was the growing notion that Finney would come out of Indo-

MY FRIEND EGON

China and head straight for Antibes before the summer was half gone and it was planned, of course, that Egon should meet him there. It was first suggested that I act as Egon's escort on his return to the Riviera. Instead, I took Harpo Marx who (by a narrow margin) does play better bridge.

If I declined the honor, it was certainly not for fear of Egon's getting lost while in my charge. You do not even have to tether Egon, for if only you will give him his leash to take charge of, he regards it as a point of honor to pretend that he is tied up.

It is, however, comparatively easy to steal him if you happen to know his one weakness. He will get into any automobile. But once that has been accomplished, the thief's troubles are only beginning. For it just is not possible to own Egon inconspicuously. More than once a taxi driver, in discharging a fare, has noticed with surprise and pleasure that a large and obviously valuable police dog has stepped quietly in through the still open door and settled himself on

the seat as though affably waiting to be driven somewhere. You could easily imagine the sequence of thoughts which then visits that driver. Probably his first impulse is to turn down his flag and ask what address. His second, perhaps, is to howl with fear. His third is to drive quietly home and present the creature to the wife and kiddies. It is then that misgivings come, for you cannot even take Egon as far as the nearest lamp post without drawing a crowd. And when, as has happened several times, his mysterious disappearance is broadcast over the radio, he is instantly and even thankfully returned, with some implausible story about having been found astroll in Long Island City.

Nor, if I declined him as a traveling companion for the voyage, was it because he is any nuisance to have around. Indeed, he can be a positive convenience. For instance, you could meet any one you wished to on the boat merely by taking Egon for one turn around the promenade deck. He has been Massa Ben's entire social credentials for some years past and he has done even more for him than that. Once when Finney lost his passport and had to get across three pesky little frontiers without one, he and Egon would merely descend from the train on the wrong side while the other passengers were docilely filing through the inspection line. Each time when sundry officials noticed this evasion and bustled importantly forward to investigate it, Finney would just whisper some magical word in Egon's ear and Egon would leap murderously forward, in the manner and with the general effect of the Hound of the Baskervilles. Each time the officials seemingly thought it best to drop the whole matter.

It was, therefore, no fear of his being a nuisance that bade me foreswear the considerable pleasure and social importance to be derived from crossing the Atlantic with Egon. I merely wished to avoid the personal grief which, sooner or later, is the inevitable portion of his every interim boss. When he is in New

York, for instance, he hangs around with William Zelcer, who owns the White Horse Tavern. They are great friends, and every morning Zelcer goes to the trouble of driving the full circuit of Central Park so that, by loping behind, Egon can get his exercise. Then Egon, to be fair about it, returns the compliment by waiting gloomily in the carriage-starter's shack outside the New York Athletic Club while Zelcer is inside getting *his* exercise. He sleeps on the floor at the foot of Zelcer's bed at the Hotel Hawthorne and sometimes, when he is very crafty, on the bed itself, although it is no easy task for him to hoist his vast and guilty bulk onto the counterpane without being noticed. He keeps patiently trying, however, and, as I have said, he is good enough to look after things in the coatroom at the Tavern.

But just let Massa Ben drop in from the other side of the world and Egon will cut Zelcer dead on the street, and, if there should be the regrettable *contretempts* of a meeting at some party, he will growl ominously and show his fangs in order to make it a matter of record (to Zelcer, to Finney and to whomever it might concern) just where his affection, like those of Verdun Belle for her Marine, are centered, for better, for worse, for richer, for poorer, in sickness and in health—world without end.